LEVEL 2 READER

D0661294

# Chasing Rainbows

By Jenne Simon
Illustrated by Prescott Hill

**SCHOLASTIC INC.**

ISBN 978-0-545-60803-9

12 11 10 9 8 7 6 5 4          14 15 16 17 18 19/0

Designed by Angela Jun

Printed in the U.S.A.         40

First printing, January 2014

It was a rainy spring morning in Lalaloopsy Land. April Sunsplash, Cloud E. Sky, and Spot Splatter Splash were spending the day inside.

"I wish the rain would stop," Cloud E. said.

"Me, too," said April. "But I'm having a great time inside with you and Spot!"

"Rainy days are good for art projects," said Spot.

Cloud E. had to agree. She and her friends
had painted some very pretty pictures.

The rainbow in April's painting was chasing
away her gloomy mood.

Soon the girls were ready to begin painting new pictures.

"I think I'll paint the rainy day," said Cloud E.

But when she looked outside, she saw something surprising.

The rain had stopped. The sun had come out. A beautiful rainbow stretched across the sky!

"I love rainbows because they're so bright and colorful," said Spot.

"I love them because they fill the sky with wonder," said Cloud E.

April smiled. "I love the wonderful surprises you can find at the end of rainbows," she said. "And that gives me a great idea. . . ."

"Come on, girls!" April cried. "We've got to chase that rainbow!"

April, Cloud E., and Spot hurried out the door.

"I wonder what we'll find at the end of the rainbow," said Cloud E.

"I think we'll find the most beautiful spot in Lalaloopsy Land," said Spot. "Then I can paint it!"

Outside, spring was blooming all over.
The warm yellow sun hung in the sky. It shone down on green meadows dotted with colorful flowers.

"It looks like all of Lalaloopsy Land has spotted the rainbow," said April.

"Look!" cried Spot. "The rainbow is leading us to that house!"

"Good thing we know who lives there," laughed Cloud E.

Peanut Big Top was thrilled to see her friends.
"Hi, everyone! What are you up to on this
sunshiny day?" she asked.

"We're chasing the rainbow," said April. "To see what we might find at the end."

"We thought we'd found it," said Cloud E.

"But it looks like the rainbow stretches farther than we knew," said Spot.

"Can I join your rainbow hunt?" asked Peanut.
"Of course!" her friends cheered.
"I hope we find something amazing at the rainbow's end," said Peanut. "Like an acrobatic act!"

The girls followed the rainbow down the road.
It led them straight to Blossom Flowerpot's
house.

"Have you come to help me in my garden?" Blossom asked. "It's always good to plant after a nice spring rain."

"We can't today," said Peanut.

"Why not?" asked Blossom.

"We're chasing the rainbow," said April. "To see what we might find at the end."

"We thought we'd found it," said Cloud E.

"But it looks like the rainbow stretches farther than we knew," said Spot.

"Can I join your rainbow hunt?" asked Blossom.

"Of course!" her friends cheered.

"Maybe we'll find a gorgeous flower garden at the end of the rainbow," said Blossom.

Next, the rainbow led the girls to Sunny's barn. They spotted Sunny Side Up and Berry Jars 'N' Jam working in the yard.

"Want to help with our chores?" Sunny asked.
"We'd like to, but not today," said Blossom.
"How come?" asked Berry.

"We're chasing the rainbow," said April. "To see what we might find at the end."

"We thought we'd found it," said Cloud E.

"But it looks like the rainbow stretches farther than we knew," said Spot.

"Can we join the rainbow hunt?" asked Sunny.
"Of course!" her friends cheered.
"I think I know someone who can help us find what we're looking for," said Berry.

Berry and the girls followed the rainbow to Bea Spells-a-Lot's house.

"I wonder what's at the end of the rainbow," said Bea.

"We do, too," said April. "We're chasing it to find out!"

"Well, look no further," said Bea. "One of my books has the answer!"

"Guess what?" said Bea. "A rainbow is a circle. That means it doesn't have a beginning or end!"

Her friends were amazed.

"That's the most magical thing I've ever heard!" said Peanut.

Science of Rainbows

"Let's celebrate the rainbow with a picnic,"
said April.

"Great idea!" said Cloud E.

The girls put together a great picnic.
Berry and Sunny brought food from their farm.
Blossom tended to the beautiful flowers.
Spot found the perfect scene to paint.
Peanut put on an amazing acrobatic show.

"Look at that," said April. "We didn't find the rainbow's end, but everyone found what she was looking for. Plus something even better."

"What's that?" asked Cloud E.

"Our friends, of course!" said April.

Cloud E. nodded. "Even the grayest days are better when we're together!"